Iridessa, Lost at Sea

Iridessa, Lost at Sea

WRITTEN BY
LISA PAPADEMETRIOU

ILLUSTRATED BY
JUDITH HOLMES CLARKE,
ADRIENNE BROWN & CHARLES PICKENS

A STEPPING STONE BOOK™
RANDOM HOUSE 🏠 NEW YORK

Library of Congress Cataloging-in-Publication Data

Papademetriou, Lisa.

Iridessa, lost at sea / written by Lisa Papademetriou ; illustrated by
Judith Holmes Clarke, Adrienne Brown & Charles Pickens.

p. cm.

"A Stepping Stone book."

Summary: Fairies Iridessa and Tinker Bell find themselves trapped
inside a pirate's bottle, floating on the sea after their plans to use the
bottle to scare away an owl go awry.

ISBN 978-0-7364-2552-0 (pbk.)

[1. Fairies—Fiction. 2. Adventure and adventurers—Fiction.]
I. Clarke, Judith Holmes, ill. II. Brown, Adrienne, ill.
III. Pickens, Charles, ill. IV. Title.

PZ7.P1954Ir 2009

[Fic]—dc22   2008015684

www.randomhouse.com/kids

Printed in the United States of America

10 9 8 7 6 5 4 3 2 1

All About Fairies

IF YOU HEAD toward the second star on your right and fly straight on till morning, you'll come to Never Land, a magical island where mermaids play and children never grow up.

When you arrive, you might hear something like the tinkling of little bells. Follow that sound and you'll find Pixie Hollow, the secret heart of Never Land.

A great old maple tree grows in Pixie Hollow, and in it live hundreds of fairies and sparrow men. Some of them can do water magic, others can fly like the wind, and still others can speak to animals. You see, Pixie Hollow is the Never fairies' kingdom, and each fairy who lives there has a special, extraordinary talent.

Not far from the Home Tree, nestled in the branches of a hawthorn, is Mother Dove, the most magical creature of all. She sits on her egg, watching over the fairies, who in turn watch over her. For as long as Mother Dove's egg stays well and whole, no one in Never Land will ever grow old.

Once, Mother Dove's egg *was* broken. But we are not telling the story of the egg here. Now it is time for Iridessa's tale. . . .

Iridessa,
Lost
at
Sea

IRIDESSA HUMMED TO herself as she fluttered beneath the leaves of a large chestnut tree. She snapped her fingers, and sparks flew from her fingertips. The sparks twinkled briefly before they were snuffed out.

Iridessa was a light-talent fairy, and she was practicing for the Full Moon

Dance. Every time there was a full moon, the light-talent group performed an elaborate dance. All the other fairies and sparrow men came to watch the light talents swirl and spin, trailing streams of colorful sparks behind them.

The next full moon was still many nights away. Most light-talent fairies hadn't even begun practicing for the dance. But Iridessa wanted to be absolutely perfect. That was why she was already hard at work, rehearsing her part of the dance.

Iridessa spun through the air, then stopped short. She turned to watch the trail of sparkles fade into the darkness behind her. It wasn't exactly even—three sparkles had escaped from the line.

Many fairies wouldn't have noticed the wayward sparkles, but Iridessa did. She sighed. "Not quite perfect," she muttered. "Yet."

She was about to start again when she heard a flutter and a low hoot. Something with large wings flapped overhead.

Without thinking, Iridessa dove for shelter in a nearby bush. "Ow!" she whispered. Thorns scratched her arm and ripped her dress. She tried to ignore them and ducked farther into the bush.

A breeze blew across her face. Then an owl landed next to the bush. A round yellow eye peered in at her.

Iridessa didn't breathe. She knew that some owls were friendly and wise. But some weren't.

The owl hooted again, and pecked at the bush with its sharp, curved beak. Iridessa's heart pounded in her ears. Now she was grateful for the thorns on the bush! The owl wouldn't be able to get past them. It hooted again.

But as Iridessa watched, the owl hunkered down outside the bush. It kept its fierce yellow eyes trained on her. Suddenly, she understood. It was going to wait her out. She was trapped!

Just then, Iridessa had an idea. With a snap of her fingers, she sent out a streak of blinding light. The owl hopped backward, surprised. Iridessa snapped another shower of sparks. The owl blinked twice. Then it flew away.

Iridessa stayed in the bush for

several long minutes. She listened for the sound of beating wings. Finally, she poked her head out of the bush. The owl seemed to be gone.

Not looking back, Iridessa flew as fast as she could. She didn't stop—she didn't even slow down—until she reached the warm, familiar lights of the Home Tree.

"All-fairy meeting!" Iridessa shouted as she flew down the hallway. "In the court-yard! Right away!"

Up and down the hall, sleepy fairies fluttered out of their rooms.

Iridessa flew through each branch of the Home Tree. She banged on doors and sounded the alarm. By the time she reached the courtyard, it was packed with fairies and sparrow men. They looked tired. Many were grumbling.

Iridessa landed in the middle of the courtyard.

"What's going on?" someone called to her. "Why did you drag us out of bed?"

The fairies turned to face her, and a hush fell over the crowd.

Iridessa saw her friend Tinker Bell off to the side. Tink's arms were folded across her chest. She was tapping her foot impatiently.

"I was just attacked by an owl," Iridessa announced.

The fairies gasped.

"Attacked?" Tink repeated. "Are you sure the owl wasn't trying to be friendly?"

"We're sure," said a voice near the back. The animal-talent fairy Beck flew over and landed next to Iridessa. "Fawn and I tried to speak to the owl. We found its nest not ten frog-leaps from the Home Tree. But it wouldn't talk to us. The owl was completely wild."

The fairies buzzed with concern. A wild owl was a dangerous thing indeed. When wild owls saw fairies, they thought of them in the same way they thought of mice or moles—as a nice snack.

"Ten frog-leaps is too close," said a sparrow man named Chirp.

"So what are we going to do?" Tink asked. She loved solving problems. "Can we wait until it leaves, then move its nest?"

"Owls choose their nesting places carefully," Beck explained. "The owl would probably build another nest in the same tree."

Just then, Queen Clarion flew into the courtyard.

The queen looked around at the frightened fairies and sparrow men. "It seems we have a very serious problem," she said.

"We do, Your Majesty," Iridessa agreed. She blushed a little under the queen's steady gaze.

"We must find a way to make the owl move. What we need in this situation," the queen said, "is an organized fairy. Someone brave and clever to think of a way to get rid of the owl."

"That's exactly the kind of fairy we need," Iridessa said. Beck nodded. The fairies in the courtyard called out their agreement.

Maybe someone like Fira, Iridessa thought. *She's brave and clever. Or Rani, although she isn't very organized.*

"It seems to me that you, Iridessa, are the perfect fairy for the job," the queen finished.

"M-m-me?" Iridessa stammered.

"Good idea!" Beck said. She slapped Iridessa on the back. "Iridessa is the smartest, most organized fairy in Pixie Hollow!"

Iridessa was about to protest. But she looked out at the crowd of fairies and saw their eager, hopeful faces. Then she glanced at Queen Clarion. The queen was smiling at her. Iridessa swallowed hard. Even though she was afraid, she just couldn't say no.

"All right," Iridessa agreed. "I'll think of something."

2

IRIDESSA FROWNED AT the birch-bark
paper in front of her. She was sitting at
her desk with her chin on her hand. She
had barely slept all night. Instead, she
had been up trying to think of ways to
get rid of the owl.

There was a knock at Iridessa's door.
Without waiting for an invitation,

Tinker Bell popped her head inside.

"Tink! What are you doing here?" Iridessa asked. Tink was her friend, of course, but Iridessa had important work to do. She didn't have time for chitchat.

"Don't mind me!" Tink said. She opened the door all the way, and the scent of freshly baked cinnamon rolls wafted into the room. "Since you didn't come to breakfast, I brought you some of Dulcie's cinnamon-pecan rolls."

She placed a tray on Iridessa's desk. The tray held a pot of tea and a plate of sticky rolls dripping with gooey icing.

Iridessa blinked in surprise. She had missed breakfast? Iridessa had never skipped a meal before. In fact, she usually got to the tearoom early so that she could sit at her favorite table, the one closest to the kitchen. Whoever sat there was always the first to be served.

Iridessa's stomach gave a low rumble. She hadn't realized how hungry she was.

"Thanks, Tink," she said. It was nice of Tink to bring her breakfast. But Iridessa didn't usually eat sweet things in the morning. She always ate pumpkin-bread toast and a robin's egg omelet. Still, the cinnamon-pecan rolls smelled delicious!

"We have to keep your brain working!" Tink said.

"I could definitely use some help with that," Iridessa said. She poured herself a cup of tea and settled back into her chair. She waited for Tink to leave, but Tink didn't go anywhere. Instead, she perched at the foot of Iridessa's bed.

"Don't you have any ideas?" Tink asked.

Iridessa huffed in frustration and glanced at the list in front of her. "I have sixty-eight ideas," she said. "But I don't need sixty-eight ideas. I need one good idea."

"Maybe some of the ideas are better than you think," Tink said. "Read me your best one."

Iridessa looked at her doubtfully.

"What?" Tink demanded.

"Well, it's just that . . ." Iridessa tried to think of a nice way to say she didn't want Tink's help. It wasn't that there was anything wrong with Tink's ideas. It was just that Tink was a little too adventurous for Iridessa's taste. What if Iridessa didn't like her ideas?

"Well, you're not exactly a planning talent," Iridessa said finally.

"You aren't a planning-talent fairy, either," Tink pointed out.

Iridessa frowned. "All right," she said at last. One thing was clear—Tink wasn't going to leave until Iridessa shared an idea with her. "Here's number thirty-five. 'Surround the owl. Then make loud noises with leaf whistles and walnut drums to scare it away.'"

Tink pursed her lips. "That sounds dangerous."

"I know," Iridessa agreed. She crossed number thirty-five off her list.

"All right, what about number sixteen? 'Use smoke to drive the owl from the tree.'"

Tink shook her head. "Fire is hard to control."

Iridessa crossed that idea off her list, too. She read Tink a few more. Each one was either too dangerous, too silly, or just plain impossible.

"This isn't helping!" Iridessa crumpled the paper and tossed it into a corner of the room.

"Let me see that," Tink said. She picked the paper up and smoothed it out on Iridessa's neatly made bed.

Iridessa cleared her throat. Tink was mussing her blanket!

But Tink didn't notice. She was too

busy reading the paper. "What about this one?" she said. "Number twenty-one. 'Put a light in the tree so that the owl thinks it's always daytime.' That's a great idea! Owls only hunt when it's dark. All we have to do is figure out how to make a light. That should be easy. You're a light-talent fairy, after all."

Iridessa thought for a moment. "We could ask the fireflies and glowworms to help."

"They'll probably be afraid of the owl, too," Tink said. "Besides, even if we got every firefly in Pixie Hollow, their light wouldn't make it seem like day." Tink tugged on her bangs.

Iridessa took a bite of a cinnamon-pecan roll. "Maybe I could capture some sunbeams," she said slowly, "and put them in a bottle."

"Great idea!" Tink was so excited that her wings fluttered suddenly. She rose toward the ceiling.

Iridessa frowned. "But it would have to be a pretty big bottle."

Tink smiled brightly at her friend.

"So let's go out and get one!" she said.

Iridessa and Tink flew to the work-shop of the glass-blowing-talent fairies. Most of the fairies and sparrow men were hard at work, but Melina took the time to answer their questions.

"Sure," said Melina. She led Tink and Iridessa through the glass-blowing workshop. "We have lots of bottles."

"Really?" Iridessa watched a fairy pull a long, hollow glass rod from a white-hot oven. The glass at the end of the rod was a half-melted blob of orange. Puffing her cheeks, the fairy blew on the cool end of the rod. The orange blob began to grow into a small sphere.

Melina caught Iridessa's glance. "Believe it or not, that's going to be a

beautiful vase. Ah! Here we are. Bottles."
Pulling off her work gloves, Melina
pointed to a shelf. "This is a big one,"
she said. She took down a red bottle the
size of an acorn.

Tink and Iridessa exchanged a look.
The bottle wouldn't hold very much
light.

"Um, do you have anything—
bigger?" Tink asked.

"Bigger than this?" Melina was
clearly surprised. "Well, as a matter of
fact, we do. The biggest this talent has
ever seen! To tell you the truth, we
weren't sure what we could use it for."

She flitted over to a wooden crate
and pulled off the top. Inside was a large,
round pale blue jug. It was nestled in a

soft cushion of clover flowers. "Isn't it enormous?" Melina said, taking it out.

Iridessa sighed. The bottle was about the size of a lemon—absolutely huge by fairy standards. But it wasn't nearly big enough for what she had in mind.

After thanking Melina, Tink and Iridessa flew outside.

"There's another idea to scratch off the list," Iridessa said miserably.

"There has to be a way to get a bigger bottle," Tink insisted.

"They don't exist," Iridessa said.

"Sure they do!" Tink replied. "I've seen them."

Iridessa frowned. "Where?" she demanded.

"In Captain Hook's quarters aboard the *Jolly Roger*," Tink said. "I noticed some when I was on an adventure with the Lost Boys."

Iridessa threw up her hands. "Tink, we don't need an adventure!" she exclaimed. "We need a plan." *That is so like Tinker Bell*, she thought. *To come up with the most impractical idea ever!*

Tink crossed her arms. "I'm just saying that there are bigger bottles right here in Never Land!"

"How in Never Land could we get a bottle from Captain Hook?" Iridessa snapped. "Just think about it!"

"I am thinking," Tink shot back. "Besides, it's not as if you have any better ideas!"

"Any idea would be better than yours!" Iridessa cried. "We've already got one problem, Tink. We don't need a hundred more!" Iridessa could feel her glow starting to turn red, the way it did when she was angry. "Are we supposed to ask Captain Hook for a bottle? Or swipe it out from under his nose?" Her voice dripped with sarcasm.

"Maybe I will," Tink said. Her blue eyes glinted dangerously.

"You do that." Angry tears sprang into Iridessa's eyes. Now she was back at square one. *I've wasted the whole morning with Tinker Bell,* she thought. *And I still don't have a plan!* "I'm going back to my room to work on some more ideas."

"Fine," Tink snapped.

"Fine," Iridessa snapped back.

And the two fairies flew off in different directions.

3

IRIDESSA WENT BACK to her room and halfheartedly scribbled down some new ideas. But she felt so terrible about her argument with Tink that she had trouble concentrating. Finally, she decided she should make up with Tink. After all, Tink had only been trying to help. Even if her idea about getting a bottle from

Captain Hook was silly, it wasn't much worse than some of Iridessa's own ideas.

She ran into Beck outside the Home Tree. "Have you seen Tink?" Iridessa asked. "I need to talk to her."

"Isn't she in her workshop?" Beck said. She looked at the teakettle where Tink fixed fairy pots and pans. It was unusually silent.

Iridessa shook her head. "I just checked. She wasn't there."

"That's funny." Beck perched on a toadstool. "I bumped into her a little while ago. She was in a hurry. She said she had to get something to help you with the owl problem. How's that coming, by the way?"

"Oh . . ." Iridessa waved her hand

vaguely. "It's fine." Her mind was racing. *Tink said she had to get something to help me?* she thought.

Part of their argument floated through Iridessa's mind. *"Are we supposed to ask Captain Hook for a bottle?"* Iridessa had said. *"Or swipe it out from under his nose?"*

"Maybe I will," Tink had replied.

A chill ran through Iridessa. "Beck," she said, "which way was Tink heading when you bumped into her?"

Beck thought it over. "Hmm," she said slowly. "I was herding the baby chipmunks back toward their nest. So I guess it must have been that way."

Iridessa gasped. Beck was pointing in the direction of Pirate Cove! "Oh, no!"

"What's wrong?" Beck asked. But Iridessa was already flying away, quick as the wind.

She knew just where Tink was headed—to the *Jolly Roger*, to get a giant bottle from the pirates.

I have to stop her! Iridessa thought. *Before it's too late!*

The *Jolly Roger* loomed like a mountain off the coast of Never Land. Iridessa was startled by its size.

How will I ever find Tink? she wondered. Anger squeezed her chest. *That is just like Tink—to flutter off to a pirate ship without a plan! She probably thinks it's another adventure!*

The wind turned in Iridessa's direction, and she was surprised to hear singing. She flew around the ship and peeked over the bow. A pirate with shaggy white hair was singing a cheery song as he mopped the deck. He wore a blue-and-white-striped shirt that strained over his belly. Another pirate with beady eyes sat nearby, coiling rope. His face was twisted in a sneer. With a shudder, Iridessa forced herself to scan the deck.

Tink was nowhere in sight.

Iridessa frowned. *Tink got herself into this mess,* she thought. *I should just let her get herself out!* But Iridessa didn't move. She was mad, but she was also scared for her friend. If the pirates caught Tink . . .

All right, Iridessa, think, think, think! she told herself. *Tink said she saw bottles in Captain Hook's quarters. So that's probably where she is.*

But where are the captain's quarters? Iridessa wondered. *Bottom, or top? Front, or back?* She didn't know anything about ships.

At that moment, a tall man in a long scarlet jacket stepped through a door. There could be no doubt that this was Captain Hook. His black curls spilled from under a wide three-cornered hat. He had a long mustache. And in the place where his left hand should be, there was a fierce-looking hook.

"Smee!" he bellowed.

"Yes, Captain?" Smee answered.

"Smee, I've finished my lunch," the captain announced. He walked up the steps to the front of the ship.

Now was her chance! Iridessa darted through the door. Behind her, Smee gave a snappy salute and said, "Aye, aye, Captain!"

Iridessa heard a clatter as soon as

33

she flew into the captain's quarters. Sure enough, there was Tinker Bell. She was struggling to lift a huge bottle made of clear glass. But it was too heavy for her. She had only managed to knock it over.

Iridessa flew to her friend's side. "Quick—hide!" she whispered.

"Dessa?" Tink's blue eyes widened at the sight of her friend. Heavy footsteps sounded outside the door.

"There's no time! Get in!" Iridessa said. She shoved Tink toward the bottle's open neck. Then she pulled a napkin over the bottle and climbed in after Tink. Under the napkin, she could just make out part of the room.

It was too dark under the napkin to see Tink's scowl, but Iridessa knew it was

there. "What do you think you're—?"

Iridessa shushed her. They heard a cheerful humming. Smee came into the room, and Iridessa watched as he shook his head.

"Oh, what a mess!" he said. He collected the dishes from Captain Hook's desk and dumped them onto the tray beside the bottle. "And we mustn't lose this!" Smee said as he popped the cork back into the bottle. The fairies felt the bottle rise into the air. Smee was carrying away Captain Hook's lunch tray!

Smee went out onto the deck, then down many flights of stairs to the kitchen in the belly of the ship. "Dear me, where has that cook got to now?" he muttered. "Ah, well. I'm the first mate, not a dishwasher. Let the kitchen boy take care of it!"

The humming and footsteps receded. The fairies waited for a few minutes. "It's all right," Tink said. "I think the kitchen is empty. We're safe."

Iridessa breathed a sigh of relief. "Great," she said. "Now let's get out of here—before someone comes back!"

4

Tink kicked at the cork, but it didn't budge. "It's stuck."

"What?" Iridessa's heart gave a flutter.

"It's stuck," Tink said again. "I can't get it out."

"Let me try," Iridessa said. She pulled Tink aside and tried to push the cork out of the bottle. It held fast.

"It's stuck," she told Tink.

"I just said that," Tink grumbled.

"Okay, let's think." Iridessa paced as well as she could at the bottom of the bottle. "Why don't we just fly?"

"While we're inside the bottle?" Tink asked.

"Sure! When we get back to Pixie Hollow, the other fairies can get the cork out." Iridessa fluttered up and placed her palms against the top of the bottle. "It's worth a try."

"Okay." Tink pressed her hands against the glass, too. "One . . . ," she said. "Two. Three!"

The two fairies fluttered with all their might. But the bottle didn't move.

Tink's face was pink with effort.

"Well," she puffed, "that . . . didn't . . . work. Got any more ideas?"

Iridessa strained to catch her breath. "What about you?" she shot back. "It's your fault we're stuck here!"

"My fault?" Tink cried. Now her glow turned pink, too.

"You're the one who had to get a bottle from Captain Hook!" Iridessa cried.

"Well, you're the one who thought of it!" Tink snapped.

Just then, the fairies heard footsteps again.

"Quick!" Tink said. She crouched and pressed her hands against the curved side of the bottle. "Push!"

Iridessa didn't have time to ask what they were doing. She just joined Tink and pushed. The bottle rolled forward, then stopped. It was stuck against the lip of the tray.

Behind them, the door creaked.

"Back up!" Tink commanded.

They did. The bottle rolled backward. And then, with a mighty rush, the two fairies rolled the bottle forward with as much force as they could. The bottle bounced over the edge of the tray. "Yay!" Iridessa cheered.

But the bottle kept rolling. "Whoa!" Iridessa cried. The napkin fell away, and she saw why they hadn't stopped. They were rolling down a chute. And the chute led right out a porthole!

"Stop!" Iridessa cried. But they couldn't stop. The fairies tumbled around inside the bottle as it dropped through the porthole.

Sploosh!

They landed in the water.

Right away, a wave washed over the bottle. Iridessa closed her eyes, sure this was the end. Once their wings got wet, they'd sink to the bottom of the sea.

But the bottle just bobbed to the surface.

"It's okay, Dessa," Tink said. She patted her friend on the back. "We're safe here."

Iridessa opened her eyes. The bottle was half in, half out of the water. On the other side of the glass, the sea was up to their waists. But inside, they were perfectly dry.

"I wouldn't exactly say we're safe," she muttered.

"Iridessa, look," Tink said. She crouched at the bottom of the bottle. A school of pretty blue and yellow Never minnows swam by. To the right, a silvery jellyfish with trailing purple tentacles floated peacefully.

Iridessa shut her eyes again. Looking at so much water was making her seasick. She was a very brave fairy, but she had her limits. "Stop watching the fish and help me think of a way out of here."

Tink stood up and checked the cork. "Maybe you could stand on my shoulders and try pushing it out again," she suggested.

Tink laced her fingers together to

give Iridessa a boost. "Wait," Iridessa said. "What will we do if I get the cork out of the bottle?"

Tink looked confused. "We'll fly away, of course."

"But what if a wave breaks over us before we can get out of the bottle?" Iridessa asked. "Our wings will get wet. We won't be able to fly back to shore."

Tink put her hands on her hips. "Are you saying we should give up?" she demanded.

"No," Iridessa replied. "I'm saying we need a plan."

"What we need," Tink shot back, "is to get out of here. That's the plan."

Iridessa rolled her eyes. *Some plan!*

"Would you quit worrying?" Tink

said. "Let's take this one problem at a time—starting with this cork!"

"Shhh!" Iridessa said. She strained her ears, trying to hear something out in the waves.

"Don't shush me," Tink snapped.

"Listen!" Iridessa said. "Do you hear that?"

The two fairies held perfectly still. Suddenly, Tink's face went pale. Iridessa knew that Tink had heard it, too—a steady *ticktock, ticktock*.

"What is it?" she asked Tink.

Tink slowly turned to look behind her. Iridessa followed her gaze—and found herself staring at a huge eye set in scaly green skin.

"It's the crocodile!" Tink cried, just

as the reptile's enormous snout opened
to show rows of sharp white teeth.

There was no escape! The fairies
watched in horror as the crocodile's jaws
closed around them.

5

"Where are we?" Iridessa asked. She could barely make out Tink's face in the darkness. The only light came from their fairy glows.

Iridessa snapped her fingers and blew gently on the spark. The spark flickered, then grew into a bright light.

"We're *inside* the crocodile," Tink

said in awe. "He swallowed us whole!"

Iridessa looked around. The belly of the crocodile was full of strange objects. She spotted a brass candlestick, a teddy bear, a hairbrush, and a straw hat. "This crocodile will swallow anything," she remarked.

"Including that alarm clock," Tink said, pointing to the clock. It was red, with a round face. It let out a steady *ticktock, ticktock.*

"So that's where the sound comes from," Iridessa said.

Tink sat at the bottom of the bottle. "Yes. Peter Pan always said, 'To watch out for the croc, just listen for the clock.' It warns you when he's nearby."

"The warning didn't do us much

good," Iridessa said. She squeezed her eyes shut. A tiny silver tear trickled down her cheek.

Tink touched Iridessa's arm. "It's okay," she said. "We'll find a way out."

Despite her words, Iridessa could tell from the look on Tink's face that she was scared, too.

Suddenly, the bottle shifted and rolled forward.

"What's happening?" Iridessa cried.

"I don't know!" Tink yelled back.

The crocodile's jaws opened. Daylight poured in, along with a flood of seawater and an old boot. A second later, the crocodile shut his mouth and it was dark again.

The boot rushed toward the fairies.

It rammed against the bottle. "Hold on!" Tink yelled. The bottle spun.

"There's nothing to hold on to!" Iridessa cried. She braced her arms against the sides of the bottle as it crashed into something.

A deafening ring—like the sound of a hundred bells—filled the crocodile's belly.

"It's the alarm clock!" Tink shouted. "I think we set it off!"

The croc's belly gave a sudden lurch. His mouth opened, letting in daylight again. The bottle—and all the other junk in the crocodile's belly—floated toward the front of the crocodile's jaws. His mouth closed, and the bottle washed backward.

"I think he's got the hiccups," said Iridessa. She turned to look at the alarm clock. It had come to rest against the crocodile's side. The bells at the top of the clock were buzzing, tickling him.

The crocodile's belly lurched again. His mouth opened, and the bottle swept forward. But just when Iridessa thought they would wash out of the croc, the neck of the bottle banged into a row of white teeth. The crocodile's jaws snapped shut again. The bottle washed back toward the center of his belly.

"Quick, Tink!" Iridessa cried. "To the back of the bottle—I've got an idea!"

There was no time to explain. Tink and Iridessa rushed toward the rear of the bottle and pressed all their weight against its bottom. The neck popped up a little bit. Iridessa hoped that it was enough.

On the next hiccup, the bottle washed forward. But this time, they were ready. The neck of the bottle was tilted upward, just enough that the bottle floated past the croc's teeth—and right out of his mouth!

The crocodile looked at the bottle in surprise. Then his yellow eyes narrowed. He opened his jaws wide.

"He's going to swallow us again!" Iridessa cried.

Hiccup!

The crocodile hiccupped three times in a row. Each hiccup pushed the bottle farther out of his reach. Finally, with a snap of his enormous green tail, he turned and swam off.

The fairies sat very still, breathing hard. Iridessa blinked in the bright daylight. Overhead, three white seagulls glided past. The sky was a deep shade of blue.

A slow smile spread across Tink's face. "Well," she said, "that was some adventure, wasn't it?"

Iridessa couldn't believe what she was hearing. "Adventure?" she shouted. "You call that an adventure? We were eaten alive by a crocodile! And we're out in the middle of the sea!"

"We're not that far from shore," Tink said. She pointed into the distance. They could see a stretch of white sand

and green palms. "Something is bound to come along and help us."

Iridessa folded her arms across her chest. "Something—like what?"

"I have no idea," Tink said. "That's what makes it an adventure."

"You really are impossible!" Iridessa cried, throwing up her hands. "The only thing that will get us out of here is a good idea. And in order to think, I need quiet. So don't talk to me. You sit on that side of the bottle, and I'll sit on this one." Iridessa plopped herself down with her back to Tinker Bell.

"What am I supposed to do?" Tink asked.

"Anything you like," Iridessa said. She put her hands over her ears.

Tink sat down, too. Now the fairies were back to back. Tink started to hum a tune.

"I can't think while you're humming," Iridessa said through gritted teeth.

Tink sighed. She turned and looked at Iridessa over her shoulder. Finally,

she asked, "Do you have an idea yet?"

"No," Iridessa snapped.

"Oh, look!" Tink said. She jumped to her feet, making the bottle sway. "A turtle! Maybe he can help us!"

A turtle with a large hooked beak was swimming past them a few feet away. "Over here!" Tink shouted. She tapped against the glass.

"Over here!" Iridessa chimed in. She tried to get the turtle's attention by snapping and sending up a shower of tiny sparks.

The turtle turned slowly toward the fairies. He looked at them curiously.

"We need help!" Tink shouted through the glass. But the turtle just kept staring.

"Could you push us to shore?" Iridessa asked. "We're trying to get back to Never Land!"

The turtle was silent.

"He doesn't understand what we're saying," Iridessa said. *If only we had Fawn with us,* she thought, *or one of the other animal-talent fairies!*

"Help us!" Tink cried. She pounded her fist against the glass. "Help!"

But the turtle was already turning away.

"No!" Tink cried. "Don't go!"

As the turtle swam off, his rear flipper knocked the bottle. The shore in the distance grew smaller and smaller, while the bottle floated farther out to sea. . . .

6

THE BOTTLE HAD been bobbing along for hours. Across the water, the sun dipped to the horizon. The sky turned gold, then pink, then purple. Night fell, the moon rose, and the two fairies were still in the bottle, out at sea.

Tink stretched out on the bottom of the bottle and fell asleep. But Iridessa lay awake for a long time, looking up at the stars and trying to ignore Tink's snores. She couldn't stop thinking about the owl and the fairies in Pixie Hollow. The fairies would be safe tonight. They had scouts to watch out for the owl. But she knew that everyone must be wondering where they were.

Queen Clarion asked me to come up with a way to get rid of the owl, Iridessa thought miserably. *And instead, I disappeared! Everyone probably thinks I gave up and ran away.*

Iridessa sighed heavily. She had given her word that she would find a solution to the owl problem. And she had let everyone down.

Iridessa lay thinking most of the

night. At some point, she drifted off to sleep. When she opened her eyes, the clouds at the edge of the sky were glowing orange. All around the bottle, the water shimmered and twinkled. The sun was rising.

Tink sat up and rubbed her eyes. "Wow," she said when she saw the clouds. "Beautiful!"

Iridessa wished she could enjoy the view. But her heart was too heavy—and she was starting to feel hungry.

The sun was halfway up the sky when a white-capped wave came along. It pushed the bottle into a fast-moving current.

Tink leaned on her hands and knees, looking out the front of the bottle as they zipped along. A school of flying fish swam next to it. They shot into the air playfully and splashed down beside the bottle.

"We're finally getting somewhere!" Tink cried gleefully.

"Yeah, but where?" Iridessa asked.

"We're going to wash up on shore. See?" Tink said. "The beach is getting closer and— Oh, look, the fish are swimming away!" The school of fish darted suddenly to the right. Tink waved merrily.

"Tink!" Iridessa shouted. "Watch out!"

Both fairies let out a cry. Their bottle was headed straight for a giant rock! The current pounded against the rock, sending foam and spray into the air. The bottle would be smashed! Iridessa squeezed her eyes shut.

But the crash never came.

Iridessa opened one eye, then the other. She was startled to find herself face to face with a beautiful creature. The creature was as big as a Clumsy, but far lovelier. She had long, blue hair and eyes the color of pale violets. Iridessa looked down and saw that the creature had a fish's tail.

"A mermaid," Tink whispered.

Iridessa had heard stories about mermaids. She knew they were unkind and vain. Still, she thought the mermaid was very pretty.

The mermaid stared through the

glass at the fairies, her head cocked to one side.

"What has the sea brought us, Numi?" asked another mermaid in a voice as light and musical as a silver bell.

Another beautiful face peered over Numi's shoulder. This mermaid had brilliant green eyes—like spring leaves after rain—and yellow-green hair.

"It's a mystery," Numi said. She gave the bottle a slight shake. The fairies stumbled against the glass.

Iridessa tapped on the glass. "Miss Mermaid," she said politely, "we'd be grateful if you didn't do that."

Numi nearly dropped the bottle in surprise. "Oola, it talks!"

"Let me see," Oola said. She took

the bottle from her friend and frowned at the fairies. "Oh!" she cried. "I know what these are—they're fairies. I used to have one. But mine didn't have wings. And it didn't come in a glass cage."

"What did you do with it?" Numi asked.

Oola shrugged and handed the bottle back to Numi. "Nothing," she said. "It was very boring."

"Boring!" Tink squeaked indignantly.

"Hey! Hey!" Iridessa tapped on the glass. "We're not boring! If you let us out, we'll show you!"

Numi tossed her long, blue hair over one shoulder. "What can you do?" she asked.

Tink rolled her eyes. "Don't bother,

Iridessa," she said. "Mermaids don't care about anyone but themselves."

But Iridessa wasn't listening. She snapped her fingers, sending up a silver spark. Then she sent up another, and another. Soon the bottle was swirling with sparks.

"Oooooh," the mermaids said, their eyes wide.

Numi smiled. "Very pretty."

Oola frowned. "My fairy never did that."

"What can the other one do?" Numi asked. She turned her violet gaze toward Tinker Bell. Tink stuck out her tongue. She put her thumbs in her ears and waggled her fingers.

"Tink!" Iridessa nudged her friend.

"Stop that! Maybe they can help us!"

Numi giggled. "That one's funny!"

"I think she's rude. Let's get rid of her," Oola suggested. "But keep the other."

"Oh, I like them both!" Numi said brightly. "I could put the bottle by my bed. It would make a nice lamp."

"A lamp?" Iridessa cried. "Hey, no— wait! You need to let us out of here! We have to get back to Pixie Hollow to save the other fairies from an owl!"

"But then you'll fly away," Numi said reasonably.

"Well, of course we'll fly away!" said Iridessa. "Weren't you listening? We have to go help our friends."

"You fairies don't understand how lucky you are." Numi wagged a finger at them. "You're going to live at the bottom of the Mermaid Lagoon in a beautiful castle!"

Iridessa gasped. "B-b-bottom of the Mermaid Lagoon?" They would never escape from there! They couldn't possibly swim to the surface.

"We have to do something!" Tink whispered.

Iridessa nodded. The mermaids had liked her show of sparks. Maybe they would like something else that glittered. Beyond the rock, sunlight sent sparkles shimmering like diamonds over the water. Iridessa concentrated, drawing two sparkles together. Then three. Then four. Then three more. The sparkles joined like petals on a flower. They floated toward the rock, a water lily of light.

Oola scooped it up. "What is it?" she asked. Then she tucked the glittery flower into her hair. "Aren't I beautiful?"

Numi frowned. "Give me that," she said.

"Why?" Oola demanded.

"Because my fairy made it, that's why," Numi said.

"I won't," Oola said. "It would look silly in your hair, anyway."

"But it's mine!" Numi insisted. She reached for the glitter flower. And as she reached, she dropped the bottle.

Once again, the fairies landed in the water with a splash. But now they were on the other side of the rock, out of the current.

Gradually, the mermaids' argument faded into the distance behind them. Iridessa sat down next to her friend. "Tink, do you think they'll come after us?" she asked.

"No. They've probably forgotten us already," Tink said.

7

THE BLUE WATERS of the Mermaid
Lagoon drifted into the distance. The
bottle was bobbing out to sea again—
this time in the wrong direction. It was
headed away from Never Land.

"I'm hungry," Tink moaned. She
and Iridessa sat facing each other. Their
backs were pressed to the sides of the

bottle. "I wonder what Dulcie served for lunch today."

Iridessa's stomach gave a low growl. "Probably mushroom tartlets," she said. Mushroom tartlets were one of her favorite dishes.

"Or cherry tomato soup," Tink suggested. "Or lemongrass salad."

"Maybe it was crab-apple sandwiches with mint sauce," Iridessa added. A shy flitterfish swam close to the bottle. Iridessa touched the glass, right where the fish's nose was, and it fluttered away in a swirl of bubbles.

"With honey cupcakes for dessert." Tink sighed at the thought of the sweet, crumbly treats, drizzled with fresh honey. "And rose-hip tea."

Iridessa rested her head against the glass. Until that moment, she hadn't realized just how thirsty she was. "We have to get out of this bottle," she said. A flicker of fear leaped in her heart. She didn't like the feeling. Light-talent fairies were usually warm-blooded and fiery—but now, Iridessa shivered. "If we don't get out soon . . ."

She didn't need to finish the sentence. Tink nodded. "I know."

If they didn't get out soon, they could be in real danger.

Suddenly, the bottle tipped and swayed. Iridessa looked up and saw a huge green wall of water. Before she had time to think, the wave crashed down over the bottle.

White foam swirled beneath them, and the bottle shot forward. The wave roared in their ears. Then, in an instant, the wave stretched out and quieted to a hiss. It washed them onto a clean stretch of white sand dotted with bubbly green seaweed. The wave retreated to the sea with a delicate swish.

Iridessa looked around. "Where are we?" she asked. In one direction, as far as she could see, white sand met blue water. In the other direction stood a lush forest. Tall, slender trees dripped with flowery green vines. Iridessa admired their pink-gold blossoms—she'd never seen such flowers before!

Tink grabbed her friend's arm. "Dessa," she said. "Did you see that?"

She pointed to something just over Iridessa's shoulder.

Iridessa turned to look. "It's just a hole in the sand," she said.

Tink narrowed her eyes at the hole. "Something moved," she whispered.

Sure enough, after a moment a long, spidery leg poked out of the hole, followed by a pretty shell. The shell was brilliant blue and looked like an oval stone. It was also very large.

"What is it?" Iridessa whispered back.

"I have no idea," Tink said.

The two fairies stood perfectly still, watching the shell. Another long, blue leg poked out, then two large pincers. Between the pincers was a small head with round black eyes, as shiny as ripe blackberry seeds. The creature was a crab.

"Hey, you!" Tink called to the crab.

Right away, the crab tucked himself back into his hole.

"I think he's afraid of us," Iridessa said. It was amazing that something with such large claws could be afraid of two fairies trapped in a bottle!

Tink's eyes were gleaming. "Yes— but he can help us! Hey!" she shouted. "Come back!"

"Stop shouting!" Iridessa cautioned. "You're scaring him!"

"Hey!" Tink shouted again. She pounded on the glass with her tiny fist.

Suddenly, a blue leg poked out of the hole.

The fairies looked at each other.

Tink tapped at the glass again. *Clink, clink, clink!*

Slowly, two antennas felt their way out from beneath the shell. Then the crab poked his head out. He looked at the fairies with his bright eyes.

Tink tapped lightly on the glass.

The crab scuttled closer on his long legs and waved a pincer, almost in greeting.

"It's okay," Tink said gently, tapping on the glass. "We're your friends."

The crab edged right up to the bottle. His beady eyes stared at it. Tink moved toward the bottle's neck, tapping all the way. "We need to get out of here," she begged the crab.

All at once, as if the crab understood, he clamped the cork in his giant pincer. With a twist and a pop, the cork came free.

Fresh air blew into the bottle. It smelled of the sea and of the pink-gold flowers. Air had never smelled as sweet to Iridessa. "Thank goodness!" she cried. She crawled out of the neck of the bottle and plopped down onto the sand. Then she gave her wings a huge stretch. They were stiff and sore.

"We're free!" Tink yelled. She followed Iridessa out of the bottle. She dropped next to the crab and planted a kiss on top of his blue shell. The crab began to scuttle away as she turned a somersault in the air.

Iridessa did a loop-the-loop. The wind against her face and her wings felt so good! Laughing, she darted toward the waves. She dipped a toe in, and then raced back to shore before the water caught her.

Tink stopped her somersaults and landed on the sand in front of Iridessa.

"Now all we have to do is get the bottle back to Pixie Hollow," she said. Her face was pink, and she was smiling.

Iridessa's smile vanished. She had forgotten that they couldn't just fly back to Pixie Hollow. They had to take the bottle with them!

"How are we going to do that?" she asked.

Tink gave her a huge grin. "I've got an idea."

8

Iridessa pushed the cork back into the bottle's neck. "I can't wait to hear this one," she muttered.

"Dessa, the answer is obvious!" Tink said. She waved a hand at the clear glass. "All we have to do is use the bottle as a boat. Look how far we've already traveled!"

Iridessa shuddered. "I'm not getting back in that bottle," she said. "No way."

"Not *in* it," Tink corrected. "*On* it. We'll ride it the way the pirates travel on their ship. It will be a fairy *Jolly Roger*!" Tink grabbed a twig and sketched her idea in the sand so that Iridessa could see. "We'll put the bottle on its side," she explained. "Then we'll tie floats to either side to keep it from spinning. We can use a stick as our mast."

"A mast?" Iridessa said. "What about a sail?"

Tink pointed to the forest behind Iridessa. The pink-gold flower vines were covered with large leaves. "There." Tink tugged on her bangs, thinking hard. "But what can we use for floats?"

Iridessa snapped her fingers, sending out a silver spark. "What about that seaweed on the shore?" she asked. "Each strand has lots of little air pockets in it."

"Iridessa, you're a genius!" Tink cried. "All right, I'll make the mast and the floats."

"What can I do?" Iridessa asked.

"Braid some rope," Tink said. "We're going to need lots."

The fairies got to work. Iridessa looked closely at the pink-gold flower vines and found that they were made of many slender tendrils. She yanked several down and started braiding them together.

Before long, she had a large pile of rope. She brought it to Tink, who was

weaving a thick mat of seaweed. Tink measured the rope. "We'll need more," she said.

"More?" Iridessa asked. But she went back to the forest to collect more vines.

By the time Iridessa returned, Tink had used the rope to tie the seaweed firmly to the bottle. She had crossed two big twigs to hold the leaf sail. Then she had used some sticky sap and a pinch of fairy dust to attach the sail to the bottle.

"It's beautiful!" Iridessa said.

Tink beamed proudly. "Not bad," she said, "considering neither one of us is a boat-making talent."

"It looks done," Iridessa said. She held out her rope. "So what's this for?"

Tink shrugged. "I don't know yet," she said.

Iridessa frowned. "You don't know yet?" She planted her hands on her hips. "I made all that rope for nothing?"

"Not for nothing," Tink told her. "I just don't know what for yet. But I once heard a pirate say that you can never have enough rope."

Iridessa's glow flared, but she forced herself to take a deep breath. After all, they didn't have time to argue. They had to get back to Pixie Hollow!

"All right," she said. "Let's get this boat into the water."

"I'll sit at the front," Tink said. "To navigate."

"What will I do?" Iridessa asked.

"Fly behind and steer," Tink said. "You'll have to push the boat in the right direction."

"Why do *I* get the hard job?" Iridessa demanded.

"Because *I* made the boat," Tink said.

"I made the rope!" Iridessa shot back. "We should take turns."

Tink gritted her teeth. "Fine."

"Who'll go first?" Iridessa asked. Just then, she noticed a flat white disk near Tink's feet. "We can flip this sand dollar," she said, lifting it out of the sand.

One side was perfectly smooth, and the other had a star pattern. "I call star," Tink said quickly.

Iridessa fluttered into the air, then
tipped the sand dollar so that it tumbled
down onto the sand. The sand dollar
landed star side up.

"Star!" Tink shouted, leaping into
the air. "I navigate first!"

Iridessa sighed. It figured. Since
yesterday, she had been trapped in a

bottle, swallowed by a crocodile, nearly kidnapped by mermaids, and cast away on a desert island, and now she had to push a bottle halfway to Never Land. She was starting to think her luck would never return.

9

Tink and Iridessa struggled to get the bottle back into the water. Time after time, the fairies had to shoot high into the air as a wave threatened to crash down on them. Then they darted back to the bottle to try again to haul it over the waves. But once their bottle-raft was safely past the breaking waves, a gust of wind picked up behind them. The leaf sail puffed out as it caught the breeze.

Iridessa guided the bottle as she fluttered along behind it. *This isn't so hard,* she thought.

"More to the right!" Tink called from the bottle's neck.

Iridessa shoved her left shoulder against the bottle. It twisted slightly in the opposite direction.

"Perfect!" Tink cried. She gave Iridessa a huge smile over her shoulder.

Iridessa grinned back.

After a while, the fairies changed places. Riding at the front of the bottle was much better. When Iridessa was behind the large leaf sail, it was impossible to tell where she was going.

Now she could see land at the horizon. She saw tall white cliffs and a shimmering waterfall. Far to the left was a tiny speck of a ship—the *Jolly Roger*. If they stayed on course, they would reach the mouth of Havendish Stream. Then they could sail down the stream all the way to Pixie Hollow.

Sooner than she would have liked, it was time to trade places again. Iridessa noticed right away that the bottle seemed heavier than before.

She checked the mast. The leaf sail fluttered, then went limp.

"What happened?" Iridessa asked.

Tink flew to the top of the sail. She licked her finger and held it up to test the breeze. "The wind has died down," she said. "We'll have to push instead."

Iridessa strained her wings. The bottle was moving slowly. It was difficult to steer, too.

Suddenly, a wave knocked the bottle-boat off course. "Tink!" Iridessa cried. "Help!"

Tink flew to the back of the bottle, and the two fairies fought to turn the boat in the right direction. Once they had it back on course, they fluttered their wings like butterflies in a windstorm. They pushed the bottle with all their strength.

Iridessa's wings ached. Drops of sweat broke out on her forehead. Her breath came in short gasps.

Tink and Iridessa had been struggling

along this way for several minutes when Tink noticed a strange shape swimming beside them. "It's that turtle!" she cried.

Iridessa stopped and turned to look where Tink was pointing. Sure enough, it was the turtle they had seen earlier.

"He's about to pass us," Iridessa said. Hot tears stung her eyes. "Tink, we're going too slowly. We'll never get back to Pixie Hollow in time!"

"I have an idea," Tink said. She flew to the base of the mast, where she had stored the rope. "He may not have helped us get out of the bottle. But he's going to help us get the bottle going!"

"What are you doing?" Iridessa called.

Tink had already tied one end of the

rope around the middle of the bottle. She made a loop at the other end, then flew to the turtle. She dropped the loop over his neck.

The rope between the turtle and the bottle stretched tight. It was working! The turtle was pulling them along toward Never Land. And he didn't seem to mind a bit. In fact, he didn't seem to notice.

Tink frowned. "We're still moving slowly," she said.

"True," Iridessa agreed. "But it's faster than we *were* going." A small smile twitched at the edge of her mouth. "And at least the rope came in handy."

Tink grinned. "I told you it would."

Iridessa tried not to watch the sky

as the turtle swam toward Never Land. She couldn't make the bottle move any faster. All she could do was be patient. She and Tink sat near the front of the bottle. The shores of Never Land grew larger as they got closer. After a while, a seagull wheeled overhead.

That's a good sign, Iridessa thought. *Seagulls like to stay near shore.* Soon they were close enough to hear the rumble of the surf.

"Tink," Iridessa said, "does it look as if the *Jolly Roger* is getting bigger?"

"Oh, nuts and bolts! That's just what I was thinking," Tink admitted. "It means our friend the turtle isn't going toward Havendish Stream."

Iridessa sighed. "I'm afraid we're

going to have to say good-bye, then," she said.

Tink flew to untie the turtle. "He's not the friendliest turtle I've ever met," she said as he swam off.

"The turtles in Havendish Stream are much nicer," Iridessa agreed.

"Speaking of Havendish Stream . . . ," Tink said, "we'd better get moving."

Both fairies flew to the back of the bottle. They pushed with all their strength. Luckily, the breeze picked up a bit, and soon the bottle was again sailing toward the shore.

"I see it!" Tink shouted. "I see Havendish Stream!"

The clear water of the stream sparkled where it met the edge of the

Mermaid Lagoon. Iridessa was happy that there were no mermaids in sight.

Her muscles ached, and she was more tired than she had ever been in her life. But they were close now! The bottle-raft bucked as they reached the breaking waves at the shore.

"We're almost there!" Iridessa shouted. She darted to the top of the sail. "Just a little to the left!"

Iridessa was about to rejoin Tink at the back, when a large wave crashed over the bottle. Instantly, Tink was soaked. She let out a choked cry as her wet wings dragged her into the sea.

"Tink!" Iridessa dove toward her friend. She grabbed Tink's outstretched hand and pulled her from the water.

Even though Iridessa was worn out, she found the energy to haul her friend onto the sand. The next wave pushed the bottle onto the beach a few feet away from them. Tink and Iridessa lay back, breathing hard. Finally, Tink spoke.

"Dessa," she said, "I can't fly."

Iridessa swallowed to clear the lump

in her throat. How could she make it all the way to Pixie Hollow alone? The bottle was too much for one fairy!

"Iridessa!" shouted a voice.

Looking up, Iridessa saw something flying toward her at top speed. She blinked. Was she sun-dazzled from too many hours at sea?

"Beck?" Iridessa croaked.

"I've been looking for you for two days!" Beck said. "You flew off so suddenly! And then when you and Tink didn't come home last night . . ." She turned to Tink. "You're all wet!" she cried.

"How did you find us?" Iridessa asked.

"A seagull spotted you. He said that

Tink was with you, too, and that you had some crazy boat bottle—" That was when Beck spotted the bottle-raft. She let out a whistle. "What have you been up to?"

Iridessa explained about the owl, the bottle, and the pirates. She left out the parts about the mermaids, the turtle, the deserted island, and the crocodile. *I can tell Beck about that later,* she thought. *When I have more time.*

"So we have to get this bottle back to Pixie Hollow," Iridessa finished up.

"Maybe you two can push it," Tink said. "With a little fairy dust to make it lighter."

"Push?" Beck shook her head. "That bottle is huge. I think we'll need help."

She put her fingers in her mouth and whistled. In a moment, the air was full of dragonflies. There were small purple ones, large golden ones, dragonflies with red and orange specks, and a few with golden stripes.

Beck spoke to them in a language Iridessa couldn't understand. They landed on the bottle in a swarm of silvery wings and pulled it out of the sand. They settled it gently on Havendish Stream.

Beck and Iridessa helped Tink on board, then climbed onto the bottle's neck. With a loud buzzing of dragonfly wings, they began speeding through the water.

10

IRIDESSA WATCHED THE scenery streak by
as the dragonflies pulled the bottle up-
stream. Tink opened her wings, drying
them in the breeze.

All at once, Iridessa realized that the
banks of the stream were crowded with
fairies and sparrow men. "There they
are!" shouted a voice. Everyone bubbled

with questions as the dragonflies slowed and brought the bottle to a stop by the side of the stream.

"What is that thing?"

"Does it have anything to do with the owl?"

"Iridessa! We thought the owl got you! It was back again last night!"

"Tink! Where have you been?"

"I'll explain everything," Iridessa promised. "But right now, I need your help." She pointed toward the bottle. "We're going to use this to scare the owl away." Her heart fluttered and she added, "I hope," under her breath.

In a flash, thirty fairies darted toward the bottle. It took only a moment for them to unfasten it from the floats and mast. "We need to pull out the cork!" Iridessa cried.

Beck called a woodchuck over. With a quick yank of the woodchuck's large teeth, the cork came free.

Raising her hands, Iridessa caught a brilliant beam of light from the setting sun. She placed it inside the bottle. Then she reached for another sunbeam. Fira saw what she was doing and came to help. Then Luna joined them. Soon all the light talents were collecting sunbeams and placing them inside the bottle as quickly as they could.

At last, the bottle was full. Beck pushed the cork into place.

The fairies had seen parties lit with fireflies and glowworms. They had seen moonlit nights full of stars. They had even seen bottled sunbeams. But they had never before seen a light as bright as this one. It seemed even brighter a few minutes later, when the sun dipped below the horizon. Around them, the forest began to grow dark.

Iridessa's eyes were just getting used to the twilight when a sparrow landed on a branch near Beck. She twittered, and Beck twittered back at her in Bird. "The owl has left its nest," Beck told the other fairies.

"We've got to get this light into the owl's tree," Iridessa said. "Before it comes back!"

Iridessa flew into the air. "This way!" she called. Behind her, fairies lifted the light-filled bottle and carried it to the owl's nesting tree.

They placed the bottle of sunbeams right beside the owl's nest. Then they bound it in place with strong spiderweb rope. The light shone in the tree as if someone had pulled the sun down to Never Land.

"Let's just hope it works," Iridessa whispered. She felt breathless.

"It has to," Tink said. Iridessa could see that her friend's lips were set in a firm line.

Just then, a fruit bat flew past, screeching a warning.

"The owl is coming back!" Beck warned. "Everyone, hide!"

The fairies vanished behind leaves

and into flowers that had closed up for the night. Tink and Iridessa ducked into a small knothole in a nearby tree branch.

The owl fluttered to the tree and sat there, blinking in the bright light. It settled in its nest and tucked its head beneath its wing. But almost right away it poked it out again.

The owl hooted unhappily. It tried to turn its back on the sunbeam bottle, but it was no use. The owl simply couldn't relax. It blinked at the light again in confusion. Then, with a mighty down-sweep of its large wings, the owl flew off.

For a moment, the forest was silent. Then a great cheer went up. All around, the fairies came out of their hiding places.

"We did it!" Iridessa cried.

Tink beamed. "Thanks to my great idea," she said.

"What?" Iridessa frowned. She planted her hands on her hips. "Don't you mean thanks to *my* great idea?"

Tink shrugged. "You helped," she said. She gave Iridessa an impish grin. "A little."

"Tinker Bell, you never would have gotten off the pirate ship if I hadn't come to rescue you!" Iridessa shot back.

"Sure—you rescued me," Tink said, rolling her eyes. "Right into the mouth of a crocodile!"

Iridessa giggled. "We got out again, didn't we?" she pointed out. "And I got the mermaids to let us go."

"That's true," Tink admitted. She smiled. "It sure was an adventure, wasn't it?" she said.

Iridessa shook her head. "Yes," she said at last. "It sure was an adventure."

Don't miss any of the magical
Disney Fairies chapter books!

Dulcie's Taste of Magic

"That first one looks like a C," she murmured. "Then O, then M." She translated letter by letter. Then she took a pencil and leaf paper and wrote out each one.

It spelled "Comforte Cayke."

"Comfort Cake?" Dulcie said out loud. "Why, I've never heard of it."

It must be an ancient recipe, she thought. Something very old but, at the same time, new and different to her. And maybe, just maybe, it had some ancient magic to it, too.

Silvermist and the Ladybug Curse

By now, other fairies had gathered around
Silvermist. The ladybug sat perfectly still atop
the water-talent fairy's head.

"You know," a garden-talent fairy named
Rosetta mused, "there's an old superstition about
white ladybugs. They're supposed to bring—"

"Bad luck!" Iris said, screeching to a stop in
front of Silvermist.

A few fairies chuckled uncertainly. No one
took Iris very seriously. But fairies were super-
stitious creatures. They believed in wishes,
charms, and luck—both good and bad.

"The white ladybug!" Iris's voice rose
higher and higher. "It's cursed!"

Fawn and the Mysterious Trickster

Fawn gave herself a little shake. Anything could be making that noise. An animal friend, for instance, like a cricket or a moth. Fawn flew closer to the closet door.

But . . . wait a second! Were her eyes playing a trick? Or . . . had the doorknob just turned?

Great greedy groundhogs! It had! The doorknob was turning! Fawn watched it, frozen with horror. Now she knew it couldn't be an animal friend. She didn't know any animal that could turn a doorknob. Fawn backed away.

With a long, low creak, the door slowly swung open.